Addison
the April
Fool's Day
Fairy

Special thanks to Kristin Earhart

To Eleanor, who is no fool

No part of this publication may be reproduced, stored in a retrieval system, or transmitted in any form or by any means, electronic, mechanical, photocopying, recording, or otherwise, without written permission of the publisher. For information regarding permission, write to Rainbow Magic Limited, c/o HIT Entertainment, 830 South Greenville Avenue, Allen, TX 75002-3320.

ISBN 978-0-545-60538-0

12 11 10 9 8 7 6 5 4 3 2 1   14 15 16 17 18 19/0

Printed in the U.S.A.   40

First printing, February 2014

Addison
the April Fool's Day Fairy

by Daisy Meadows

SCHOLASTIC INC.

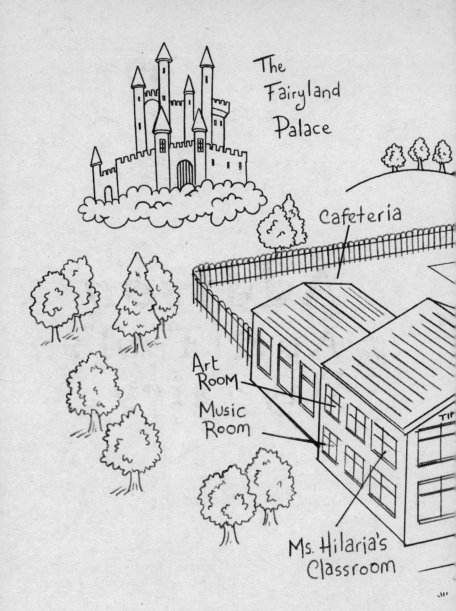

The
Fairyland
Palace

Cafeteria

Art
Room

Music
Room

Ms. Hilaria's
Classroom

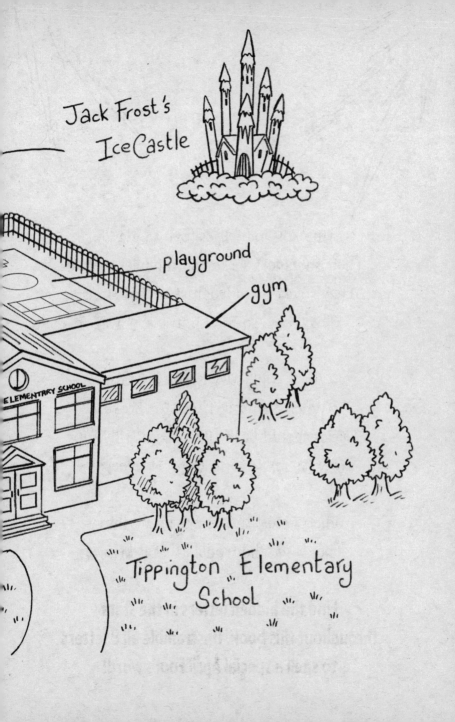

Jack Frost's
Ice Castle

playground

gym

ELEMENTARY SCHOOL

Tippington Elementary
School

Humans and fairies love to giggle.
Their shoulders shake and tummies wiggle.
They snicker and laugh at pranks all day.
They're all so foolish in every way.

April Fool's Day is one big joke.
When I ruin it, I'll go for broke.
Fairies should know it's not just silly fun.
Now it's my turn to laugh at everyone.

When I steal that fairy's magic things,
They'll see the trouble that it brings!

**Find the hidden letters in the stars
throughout this book. Unscramble all 8 letters
to spell a special April Fool's word!**

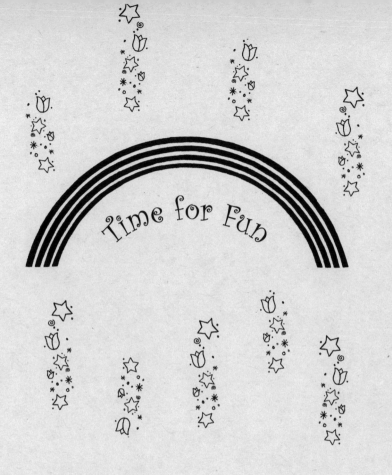

Time for Fun

Contents

The Eve of April

It was the last day of March, and Rachel Walker could not have been happier. Her best friend, Kirsty Tate, was spending the night. On top of that, Kirsty was going to school with her the next day!

"You're going to love Ms. Hilaria," Rachel insisted. "She's such a fun teacher. I think she might have some

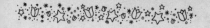

good jokes planned for April Fool's Day."

"Oh, I hope so!" Kirsty said with a smile. "I love April Fool's Day."

"Me, too," Rachel agreed.

The two girls agreed on a lot of things. They both loved a good joke. They both liked eating ice cream for a special after-school treat. They both believed in

fairies. More than that, they were both friends with the fairies!

"You know, I sometimes think Ms. Hilaria believes in fairies," Rachel told Kirsty.

"Really? Why?" Kirsty asked.

"She suggested I read a book series about fairies, and she told me that she

used to have dreams about visiting a special place where fairies lived," Rachel explained. She had a twinkle in her eye while she spoke.

"Just like Fairyland," Kirsty said. "I love when we dream about Fairyland!" Rachel and Kirsty sometimes had the same dreams. This often happened when the king and queen of Fairyland were trying to send them a message. Whenever King Oberon and Queen Titania needed help, they called Kirsty and Rachel first. Jack Frost was Fairyland's top troublemaker, and the girls had helped the fairies defeat him and his tricky goblins many times.

"I like those dreams,

too, but I like it even better when we actually go to Fairyland," Rachel admitted.

"Me, too."

The two friends smiled at each other. They knew they were very lucky to have fairy friends.

Both girls had already brushed their teeth and put on their pajamas. They settled into bed to read before they turned off the light.

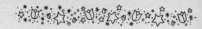

"Hey!" Rachel said with a laugh. "Are you trying to pull the first prank of April Fool's Day?" She pointed to her wall calendar.

Kirsty followed Rachel's gaze and noticed that the calendar was turned to the month of February. "No, I didn't change it," Kirsty insisted. "Besides, I know that wouldn't trick you. You'd never think it was still February."

"I wonder if it was my mom," Rachel said. "I'm going to ask her. She has to do better than that if she wants to fool me!"

Rachel marched over to her bedroom door. She had a proud grin on her face, but her playful mood changed when she couldn't turn the doorknob. "What's going on?" she asked, frowning. "The doorknob is all slippery." Rachel tried to turn it with her other hand. When that didn't work, she started to pull on the door with all her might. "Why won't it open?" she complained. "This isn't funny anymore."

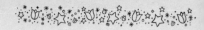

Kirsty started to worry. Were they stuck in Rachel's room? Just then, Kirsty heard a sweet giggle chime in her ears. It sounded familiar! "Rachel, did you hear that? I think it's a fairy playing a joke on you!" Kirsty said with excitement.

"Well, whoever is doing it, it's not very funny," Rachel said. She planted her feet firmly on the wood floor and yanked on the door with both hands. All at once she lost her grip and landed with a loud *thump*.

"Oh, no," a tiny voice whispered in Kirsty's ear. "It's worse than I thought."

Kirsty looked around and spotted a magical glow floating past her ear.

When the glow came to rest on the edge of Rachel's bed, Kirsty could see what she already knew: It was a fairy! The fairy buried her head in her hands. Her loose, dark curls swung forward. Even though Kirsty couldn't see her face, she knew the fairy was crying.

Goblins Are Fools

"Rachel," Kirsty whispered, "it's a
fairy!" Kirsty reached forward and gave
her friend's shoulder a nudge, but Rachel
just shook her head. Kirsty knew
something wasn't right. Rachel was
usually excited to meet a new fairy!

Kirsty quickly turned to the tiny fairy

perched on Rachel's bed. "Hello, I'm Kirsty. Can I help you?"

"It's just so sad," she said. Her face was somber, but her outfit was cheerful. She wore a sleeveless dress with pink and

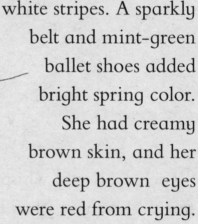

white stripes. A sparkly belt and mint-green ballet shoes added bright spring color. She had creamy brown skin, and her deep brown eyes were red from crying.

"What's wrong?" Kirsty asked.

"It's just so sad when a good joke gets ruined," she said.

"So you're the one who changed the calendar page," Kirsty replied, glancing over at Rachel, who was still

slumped by
the door.

"Well, yes," the
fairy admitted.
"But the real joke
was the slippery
doorknob. The

other fairies said that Rachel has a
good sense of humor, so I thought she'd
like it."

"Normally, she does. Is there
something strange going on?" Kirsty
asked.

"It's all Jack Frost's fault, as usual," the
fairy said with a sniff. "But I nearly
forgot my manners." The fairy sat up
straight and smoothed the wrinkles out
of her dress. "My name is Addison. I'm
the April Fool's Day Fairy."

"It's so nice to meet you. I'm Kirsty."
She looked toward the door. "This is
Rachel. Rachel, this is Addison."

Rachel shook her head. She seemed
confused. "Oh, hello," she said. "I didn't
see you there."

"Jack Frost is up to his old tricks,"
Kirsty told Rachel.

"This time, he's messing with my
favorite holiday," Addison said. "April
Fool's Day is supposed to be a fun day,
when people—and fairies—get to be a

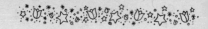

little mischievous. Everyone needs to exercise their sense of humor once in a while!" The fairy threw her hands up. "But Jack Frost doesn't want anyone to have fun this year. He has stolen my three magical objects. They help make jokes work. Without them, pranks won't be funny at all. Or worse, they could even seem mean. I need to get my objects back!"

"Of course we'll help," Kirsty quickly reassured the flustered fairy.

Rachel nodded. "Tell us about the objects," she suggested.

"The first is my magic watch. It helps people *get* jokes, so that they understand why they are funny."

13

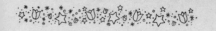

Kirsty's eyes grew wide. "Do you think that's why Rachel didn't laugh about the slippery doorknob?"

"I do," Addison replied. She gave Rachel a kind smile. "The watch also helps with the timing of jokes, which is a very important part of humor."

"What are the other objects?" Rachel asked.

 "The second one is a can of jelly beans," Addison said.

"Jelly beans?" Kirsty looked confused . . . and hungry.

"Well, it's a trick can. There's a picture of jelly beans on the outside, but when you twist off the cap, toy snakes pop out! It's a classic gag!" Addison slapped her leg as she giggled. "The jelly-bean can makes sure

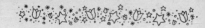

that pranks work." She took a deep
breath and sighed. "The third object is
the most magical. It's a key. It helps
people understand when the joke is on
them, and it gives them confidence to
laugh at themselves." The fairy's fingers
reached toward her neck. "I
always wear the key
right here, on a
necklace."

There was nothing
funny about that. "Jack
Frost's goblins took
all the objects while I was sleeping. Then
Jack Frost hid them in the human world.
That means we have less than a day to
get them back!"

"Don't worry, Addison," Rachel said.
"We've dealt with the goblins before.

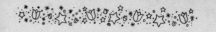

They are always losing things, and
Kirsty and I always find them. We can
help you save April Fool's Day."

"That's great news!" The fairy's eyes
began to sparkle. "Maybe we can start
by planning some great jokes for your
parents, Rachel."

"That's a wonderful idea," Rachel
agreed. "They love April Fool's Day."

With that, the three friends got started.

A Lack
of Laughs

The next morning, Mrs. Walker rushed
into Rachel's room in a frenzy. "Oh,
girls," she said, "we are late! I'm so sorry.
I overslept."

Kirsty and Rachel sat up in bed and
smiled at each other. Addison's prank
had worked! The fairy had magically
changed all the clocks in the Walkers'

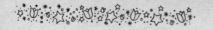

house. The clocks said 8:00, but Rachel and Kirsty knew it was still only 7:00. They had plenty of time to get to school by 9:00.

"Happy April Fool's Day!" the girls cried out, but Mrs. Walker just stared at them.

"Mom, we aren't late. We changed the clocks last night. We moved them

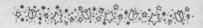

forward an hour," Rachel explained.

"But that's impossible. All the clocks in the house say it's eight o'clock," Mrs. Walker insisted, glancing at the clock on Rachel's dresser. "You couldn't have changed them *all*. Hurry! Get dressed. . . ." Her voice trailed off as she ran out of the room.

"I guess Addison's magic worked too well," Kirsty said. "Your mom can't believe all the clocks are wrong."

"She didn't think it was funny," Rachel said, sounding disappointed.

"That's because Addison's watch is missing," Kirsty reminded her friend. "Addison said that would happen. Let's get ready and see if any of our other pranks work," Kirsty said hopefully.

The girls pulled their clothes on and hurried downstairs.

"Good morning," Mr. Walker greeted them in the kitchen. "Your mom was mistaken about the clocks, so we have plenty of time for breakfast, if you're hungry."

"Sure," Rachel said. She searched her dad's face for a smile, but there was not even a hint of one.

The clock above the kitchen sink was back to the actual time, but Rachel's parents still didn't realize it had been a joke.

The girls eagerly watched as Mr. Walker reached for the sugar bowl. They had replaced the sugar with salt the night before. He put a spoonful in his coffee and stirred it.

Rachel bit her lip. Her dad took a sip and frowned. Then he sipped some more.

"April Fool's!" she called out.

"What?" Mr. Walker asked.

"It's an April Fool's joke," Rachel explained. "We switched the sugar and salt. You put salt in your coffee!"

"Huh," Mr. Walker said. "It doesn't taste that bad."

21

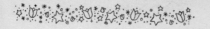

"Here, I'll pour you a fresh cup, so you can put sugar in it," Rachel offered.

"Oh, no. It's really fine," Mr. Walker said. "I like it like this." He didn't laugh or smile. He just took another swallow.

Rachel looked at Kirsty with concern. This wasn't like her dad at all! He usually loved a good April Fool's Day prank. He  laughed at his own jokes, even when they weren't that funny.

Mrs. Walker stepped into the kitchen and poured herself some cereal. Mr. Walker poured himself a bowl, too. Addison had helped the girls switch the cereals into different boxes the night

before, but Rachel's
parents didn't seem
to notice.

"My mom always
eats the nutty
granola," Rachel
whispered to
Kirsty. "And my

dad likes the Honey O's." Kirsty shook
her head as she watched Mrs. Walker eat
the O's that she had poured out of the
granola box. Mr. Walker crunched down
on the big nuggets of granola.

"How's your cereal?" Kirsty asked
when she sat down with her own bowl.

"Just fine," the Walkers said at the
same time. Kirsty thought it was kind of
spooky.

As soon as they were done eating,

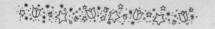

Rachel pulled Kirsty into the front hallway. "I think we should get to school," she said. "If things are this weird here, I can't imagine what's happening there."

"And maybe we'll find Addison and some of her objects," Kirsty added.

"I certainly hope so," Rachel said, "or else this will be one sad April Fool's Day."

Goblin Grumbles

"Is your school always like this?" Kirsty asked as they walked through the front doors. Kids were running in the halls and teachers were rushing around, looking serious.

Rachel shook her head. "No, it's not."

Kirsty noticed that all of the bulletin

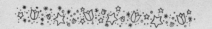

boards looked strange. Someone had
switched all the letters.

"That's not even a good prank,"
Rachel said. "Someone scrambled the
letters on the signs, but they don't say
anything. That's not funny at all."

Just then, Kirsty felt a tug on her hair.
It was Addison! "Hello, girls!" the fairy
greeted them. "Don't forget that my
watch is missing. It's hard to tell if

anything is funny
when I don't have
my watch," the
fairy whispered.

"Nothing will
be funny if someone sees you," Rachel
said in a hushed voice. "You need to
hide, Addison."

"Okay," Addison agreed, looking
around and seeing all the kids. "But
you'll look for my magic objects, right?"

"Absolutely," Kirsty assured her. "We'll
find them all before April Fool's Day is
over."

As soon as she heard this,
Addison flew down and
ducked into one of the
square pockets on the
front of Rachel's sweater.

Rachel took Kirsty's hand and gave it a light tug. "This is my classroom," she said. As soon as they entered, Kirsty knew something was wrong. All the kids were bunched together in front of the storage cubbies, grumbling.

A boy wearing a striped sweatshirt picked at the name tag above one of the cubbies. "Hi, Rachel," he said with a scowl. "Someone turned all our name tags upside down. Why would anyone do that?"

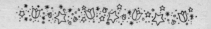

"I don't know, Aaron," Rachel said. "That's frustrating." She introduced the boy to Kirsty. Then she led her friend to the last cubby in the row. "Here's mine," she said.

Addison poked her head out of Rachel's pocket. "This prank looks like it took a long time to do," the fairy said. "It's not a bad joke, really. It's sad that no one thinks it's funny. No one's laughing at anything today."

"Well, that's because it's annoying," Rachel complained. She was trying to peel off her name tag without ripping it.

"Now that I think of it, this could be the work of the

29

goblins," Addison said. "If they are here, my objects probably are, too."

Just then, the homeroom bell went off. But it didn't sound like a bell at all. It sounded like a chicken squawking. "That's hilarious!"

Addison declared with a giggle, bouncing up out of Rachel's pocket.

"Shhh," Kirsty whispered. "You need to stay hidden or someone will see you."

Addison pouted and then ducked back into the pocket. She couldn't believe that Rachel and Kirsty hadn't laughed at the

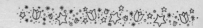

chicken bell. This was the worst April
Fool's Day ever!

Just then, Ms. Hilaria hurried into the
classroom. "I'm so sorry I'm late," she
said. "My clock was wrong this morning
and I couldn't find my watch." She
looked at the clock above the classroom
door. It said 1:30. "That's odd. This
clock is wrong, too. I wonder what's
going on." She flipped through papers on
her desk and mumbled to herself.

"Let's go up. I should introduce you to
her before class starts," Rachel suggested.
Kirsty nodded and followed Rachel up
the aisle.

As soon as Ms. Hilaria saw them, she
smiled. "You must be Kirsty," she said.
"I've heard so much about you."

"And I've heard a lot about you," Kirsty responded.

"I hope you have a great day with us," the teacher said. Then she asked Kirsty a couple of questions about her school.

As they talked, Rachel's eyes wandered around the room. There was a lot of stuff out of place. *Addison's hunch is right,* Rachel thought.

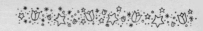

The goblins have been here. Just then, she heard a low grumble. And another. It didn't take Rachel long to spot a flash of green in the corner of the room. The goblins were still in the room! What were they doing down there? Rachel was certain they were up to no good.

A Wonderful Watch

moofapi

Rachel tried to think. What should she do? What if Ms. Hilaria discovered the goblins?

"Well, girls," the teacher said, "I need to figure out what time it is, and you need to get back to your seats."

"Of course," Kirsty agreed.

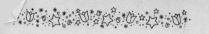

But Rachel didn't budge. "Ms. Hilaria?"

"Yes, Rachel?" The teacher looked at her curiously.

Rachel didn't respond. She glanced at the goblins hiding near the teacher's desk, hoping she could come up with a plan. "Um," she began, "just let us know if we can help at all today."

The teacher smiled. "Of course, Rachel. Thank you."

Rachel hurried to her desk. As soon as Kirsty sat down next to her, she leaned close. "Goblins!" she whispered.

"Where?" Kirsty asked.

"Near Ms. Hilaria's desk," Rachel replied.

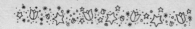

"Of course," Addison said, poking her head out from Rachel's pocket. "They probably had to hide when the kids came in the classroom. Did they have my watch?"

Rachel shook her head. "I didn't see it."

The girls looked toward the front of the classroom. Ms. Hilaria was busy searching through her desk. All at once, she stood up and called to the students. "Everyone, it's almost time for music class." She held a mint-colored watch in her hand.

Rachel felt something poke her in the side.

"Psst! Rachel, that's my watch!"

The girls looked down and noticed Addison peering over the top of Rachel's desk. "She has it!"

"The goblins must have dropped it in her desk when they were playing their pranks," Kirsty guessed.

"How will we get it back?" Rachel wondered out loud.

The three friends stared at the watch in Ms. Hilaria's hand and tried to come up with a plan. At once, they gasped. They had all seen it. There was a hand reaching out from under the teacher's desk. The hand had long green fingers — and it was grabbing at the watch!

"Oh, no," Kirsty said.

Several of Rachel's classmates turned to look at them. Addison immediately dipped down and hid inside Rachel's desk. Rachel bit her lip. She needed to think, and quick! They couldn't let the goblins get the watch!

"Ms. Hilaria!" Rachel blurted out. "That's my friend's watch!"

Now everyone turned and looked at
the teacher. Ms. Hilaria appeared
confused. "That's odd. I have no idea
how it got in my desk," she said. She
walked down the aisle and handed the
watch to Kirsty.

"Oh, thank you," Kirsty said. Of
course Ms. Hilaria assumed that the
watch belonged to Kirsty! After all,
Kirsty was Rachel's friend.

As soon as Ms. Hilaria
turned around, Kirsty
slid the watch into
Rachel's desk. She
felt a light tap on
her hand. She
knew it was
Addison, saying
thank you.

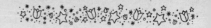

"Everyone, let's line up for music," Ms. Hilaria announced. The kids stood up and started to make a line at the door.

Rachel and Kirsty lingered. They peeked into Rachel's desk, but they couldn't see anything.

The two friends looked back at the desk as they followed the other kids out of the classroom. "I feel funny leaving Addison alone," Kirsty said, worried.

"But it looked like she wasn't there anymore," Rachel said. "Maybe she already went back to Fairyland."

Kirsty nodded. She hoped so. The group walked quietly past the principal's office and turned down a long hallway. The music room was at the very end.

Suddenly, a boy at the front of the line laughed out loud. Then the girl behind him snickered. Soon, there was a whole chorus of laughter filling the hallway.

Aaron pointed at a bulletin board and giggled. Rachel could tell it was another sign whose letters had been moved around. The sign usually said STUDENTS OF THE MONTH, and it showed the pictures of one kid from every class in the school. But the bulletin board said something very different now.

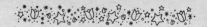

"'Hotshot Stuntmen!'" Kirsty giggled.

"That's hilarious," Rachel said, looking at all the pictures of kids in their school. "Look how someone drew bodies for the portraits. And put the people in dangerous scenes."

Kirsty looked closer and could see that two kids were jumping over a canyon on a motorcycle. It looked like another kid was climbing the Empire State Building. "The kids are still smiling, like nothing is happening at all! It really is funny," Kirsty said.

"And the best part is that everyone knows it!" said Rachel. It was proof that Addison had made it back safely to Fairyland. Now they had just two objects left to find!

Jelly-Bean
Jumble

Contents

Musical Mayhem

Kirsty and Rachel were relieved that
Addison had made it back to Fairyland.
They were so happy, it took them a
while to realize that most April Fool's
jokes were still not working.

In music class, everything seemed
normal at first, but then Rachel nudged
Kirsty with her elbow. "Do you

remember what Addison said about her magic jelly-bean can?"

"Yes," Kirsty replied. "The jelly-bean can helps make jokes work."

"So, if someone tried to pull a prank, the jelly-bean can helps everything go as planned."

"Exactly," Kirsty said.

"Then we should keep an eye on that tambourine," Rachel

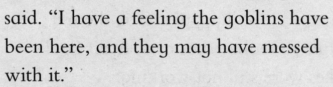

said. "I have a feeling the goblins have been here, and they may have messed with it."

Kirsty frowned, trying to figure out what her friend meant. She didn't see anything unusual.

Mrs. Bowles, the music teacher, cleared her throat. "Before the next song," she announced, "I need five of you to pick instruments."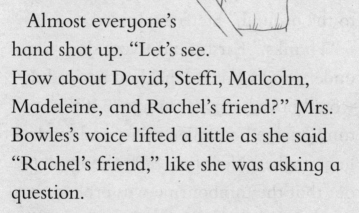

Almost everyone's hand shot up. "Let's see. How about David, Steffi, Malcolm, Madeleine, and Rachel's friend?" Mrs. Bowles's voice lifted a little as she said "Rachel's friend," like she was asking a question.

"Her name is Kirsty," Rachel called out.

"Yes, Kirsty." The music teacher smiled.

The five kids stood up and headed for the music bins. Kirsty noticed the

tambourine. She glanced back at Rachel. Her best friend nodded, so Kirsty reached for it.

"Oh, don't take that," the girl named Steffi said. "Look, it's broken. One shake and all the jingles will fall out and crash to the ground," Steffi explained.

"Thanks," Kirsty said. Now she understood what Rachel had noticed. It would have been a funny joke if the tambourine had fallen apart and made a huge racket. Now that Steffi had pointed out that the tambourine was broken, however, no one picked it up. Kirsty chose a set of bongo drums instead. As Kirsty and the other kids sat down, the teacher told the class that they would be singing "Rainbow Connection."

"Annabelle, would you like to turn the pages for me?" she asked, sitting down at the piano.

Annabelle smiled at Steffi and hurried to stand next to the piano bench. Rachel leaned over to Kirsty. "Steffi and Annabelle are best friends," she explained. "They are nice, but they don't seem to like to have fun. They just like to follow the rules. They also like to tell on other kids when they are breaking the rules."

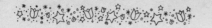

Kirsty understood. She could think of a few girls at her own school who were the same way. Kirsty always followed school rules, but she tried not to be too much of a teacher's pet.

Mrs. Bowles reached out her hands and curved her fingers over the piano keys. Just as she was about to start, Annabelle yelled. "Stop! Look! This isn't the music for 'Rainbow Connection' at all," she pointed out.

Mrs. Bowles gasped and yanked the music from the stand. "Goodness, that would have been embarrassing," she mumbled, her cheeks a nervous pink.

"It might have been embarrassing," Rachel admitted, "but it also would have been funny."

"I wonder what song she almost played," Kirsty whispered.

"I guess we'll never know, and we won't get to laugh about it."

As it was, no one had laughed in a long time—not since they saw the mixed-up bulletin board in the hallway. The kids just shifted around while Mrs. Bowles searched for the right music.

Kirsty sighed and picked up the bongo drums from the floor. As she put them on her lap, a cloud of sparkles burst from them.

"Look, Rachel," Kirsty whispered.

Addison poked her head out from the base of the drums. "We have to find my jelly-bean can. No jokes are working," she insisted. "This is no laughing matter!"

The Almost Jokes

Back in in Ms. Hilaria's classroom, Addison was anxious. She had a hard time staying still in Rachel's pocket. "What's happening now?" she whispered every two minutes, hoping the girls would have a hint of good news.

Unfortunately, there was little good news to go around. "Not much," Kirsty

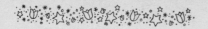

replied for the fourth time. They hadn't
seen any goblins since before music class.
There hadn't been any funny jokes,
either.

"The goblins aren't
here," Addison
pointed out.
"Why don't we
look someplace
else?"

"Because we're in school," Rachel said
in a hushed tone. "We have to stay in
class now. We can't just snoop around."

Addison sighed and tucked her wings
back into the cramped pocket.

All of the kids were working on an art
project about spring. They were using
paint, construction paper, pipe cleaners,
scrap paper, and glue. It was messy!

Kirsty had made a lovely collage of daisies and poppies. The flower petals were paper, and she had painted the stems and grass in green. "I need to clean off my paintbrush," she said to Rachel. She nodded toward the craft sink at the back of the room.

Rachel glanced toward the corner of the room. "Wait," she whispered.

"Someone is trying to play a good joke. Look at the sink nozzle."

Kirsty eyed the sink. Sure enough, she could see what Rachel was talking about. Someone had put a rubber band around the handle of the nozzle. The rubber band held the spray nozzle in the on position. The next time someone turned on the sink, the nozzle would immediately spray water. "That's a good trick," Kirsty whispered in reply. She hoped that the water didn't ruin anyone's art, but she also wanted the prank to work. Everyone had been so solemn all day—they could use a funny April Fool's Day joke to make them laugh.

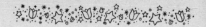

Rachel tugged on Kirsty's sleeve. "Stop staring," Rachel said under her breath. "Steffi's headed to the sink."

At once, Kirsty pretended to be working on her art project again. She watched out of the corner of her eye. She could see Steffi reach for the cold-water knob and then stop.

"Ms. Hilaria!" Steffi called. "Ms. Hilaria!"

The concerned teacher hurried over to her student's side.

"Someone was trying to play a mean trick on me." Steffi huffed. "The water would have gotten all over my shirt, and it's brand-new."

"There's no need to be alarmed," Ms. Hilaria said in a kind tone. "I think it was just an April Fool's prank. You noticed it before any harm was done. Let's take off the rubber band."

Ms. Hilaria leaned forward and made sure the sink worked normally again.

"Class, let's finish up. It's time for lunch," the teacher announced.

The students all rinsed out the

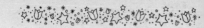

paintbrushes and placed the supplies back
in the art bins. Then they went to their
cubbies to get their lunches and their
jackets.

Rachel and Kirsty went to stand at the
head of the line. The kids filed out of the
room and down the hallway. When the
girls came to the doors that led to the
cafeteria wing, Kirsty
paused. The sign on
the door said PUSH.

Rachel went
ahead and pulled
the door open, like
she always did.

"I almost fell for
that one," Kirsty said.
She noticed now that
the PUSH sign had been

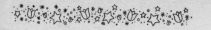

written in crayon.

"Oh!" Rachel said, looking at the sign. "I didn't even see that. I guess I just know that you pull on this door. After all, my class goes through it every day."

Addison grumbled from Rachel's pocket. "I'll be surprised if any jokes work today." The fairy's tiny mouth drooped into a big frown.

Not-So-Tasty Tricks

"Your cafeteria is so big," Kirsty commented as the friends entered the room. There were rows and rows of tables. There was a long window that opened to the kitchen. It was where the cooks served the students.

Rachel and Kirsty had packed their lunches, so they found seats and sat

down. There
were already
two boys at
the other end
of the table.
One had
wavy, dark
brown hair.

The other's hair was red, and he had
freckles. Rachel waved hello.

"They were in my class last year," she
told Kirsty.

"Why do you think they need so many
milks?" Kirsty asked her friend so that
no one else could hear.

Rachel gazed over and realized why
Kirsty had asked. Both boys had three
cartons of milk. "I don't know," she
responded. But as the girls stole glances,

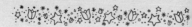

they soon figured out the boys' plan.

The boys were using the tips of ballpoint pens to poke little holes in the bottom of the cartons. As soon as they were done, they placed the cartons back on the table.

"That's pretty clever," Kirsty whispered. She could picture the milk sprinkling out like a fountain as soon as someone picked up the carton. "What do you think they'll do next?"

Rachel didn't get a chance to respond to her friend. Several girls from her grade gathered at their table and asked if they could sit down.

"Of course," Rachel said. "This is my friend Kirsty. She's visiting from Wetherbury." The other girls all welcomed Kirsty with kind greetings and big smiles. Soon they were all deep in conversation. Kirsty had forgotten about

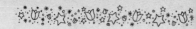

the boys at the other end of the table, until they moved down to sit closer to the girls.

"Hey! Do you want some milk?" the boy with dark hair asked.

Kirsty was surprised that his voice did not have even a hint of mischief.

The boy with freckles had a crooked smile. "Yeah," he said, "we could never drink all of this. I don't know why we bought so much."

"Sure," Kirsty said, hoping the others would also agree.

"I guess so," said Orly, whose pink ruffled shirt matched her lip gloss. She reached out for a carton. The boy with

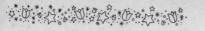

the freckles scooted it across the table.

Natasha, who had sparkling blue eyes, nodded. "Thanks," she said. "My hummus sandwich is kind of dry."

The boys smiled before going back to their end of the table. They had handed off all six of the milk cartons and were watching the girls closely.

Kirsty and Rachel watched, too. Natasha tapped a straw on the table and tore off the paper wrapper. She opened the carton and dropped the straw in. Then she lifted up the milk and took a long sip.

Kirsty watched with surprise. Nothing happened.

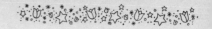

Next, Orly lifted up her carton and gave it three big shakes.

Rachel held her breath. She was sure milk would burst out of the pen holes and splash all over the table. But Orly set the milk down, opened the top, and drank from the spout without incident.

The same thing happened when Kirsty and the other girls drank their milk: nothing. At the end of the table, the boys had scowls on their faces.

"Thanks for the milk," Natasha said sweetly, but the boys only huffed.

Kirsty lifted her carton and examined the bottom. She could see the holes, but the milk wasn't coming out. She looked

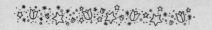

across the table
and noticed
Addison
peeking over
the edge. "Use the
secret weapon!" the fairy whispered.

The "secret weapon" was a container of cookies that Addison had given them. They were homemade chocolate sandwich cookies. They looked delicious! But Addison had used toothpaste instead of vanilla cream for the centers. It was a hilarious joke, and Kirsty was sure it would make everyone laugh at themselves.

Sandwich Creams and Jelly Beans

"Hey, everyone," Rachel announced to the table, "we brought cookies!"

She pulled the container of scrumptious-looking cookies out of a canvas bag. "I'd love to share them with you."

Rachel and the other girls at the table stared at the stack of fresh-baked goods. The chocolate cookies looked rich, and the cream in the middle looked fluffy and sweet. Rachel's mouth started watering, even though she knew the cream was really toothpaste.

"Those look amazing," Rachel said, smiling at Kirsty.

"They really do," agreed Orly. "It's too bad I'm not hungry."

"Yeah, I'm not, either," Natasha said. "That hummus sandwich was filling. But I still want a cookie. Thanks, Kirsty!" Kirsty watched as Natasha's hand hovered over the cookies. At last, she

selected a cookie with an extra-thick
layer of cream. Natasha licked her lips as
she lifted the cookie to her mouth. Just as
she was about to take a bite, the bell for
recess rang. Natasha was so startled that
she dropped the cookie. It skidded off the
table and onto the floor.

"Oh, Kirsty, I'm so sorry!" Natasha exclaimed. "Oh, well. I guess that's a sign. I didn't really need a cookie anyway."

Rachel looked at her best friend in disbelief. She knew this was because Addison's jelly-bean can was missing. No one ever turned down cookies!

Kirsty sighed with disappointment. It seemed impossible that none of the April Fool's jokes had worked. The other girls were gathering their things for recess, but Rachel and Kirsty stayed in their seats.

"Are you coming?" Orly asked.

"In a minute," Rachel replied. She

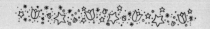

forced herself to smile before Orly and
her other school friends walked away.

"Psst."

Rachel looked down.
Addison tugged on
her sweater.

"Addison, someone
will see you!" Rachel said.

"Maybe," Addison said. "But you
need to see something, too." The fairy
pointed toward the cafeteria kitchen.

It took a minute, but Rachel realized
that the lunch ladies now had long noses
and green skin—goblins had taken over!
They were dressed the part in hairnets
and ruffled aprons. One of the goblins
was carrying a large sack with JELLY-
BEAN CANS scrawled across it.

"Kirsty, look!"

Kirsty's eyes grew wide as she took in the scene. "I can't believe they wrote that on the bag," she whispered. "They're making it easier for us."

"Nothing comes easily with the goblins," Addison warned. "It looks like that bag is full. They probably found all the cans in town. I wonder which one is mine."

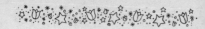

As they spoke, a goblin with extra-long fingers pulled the order window closed. The girls could hear him latch it shut. Now they couldn't see into the kitchen.

The girls tiptoed to the kitchen door and peeked inside.

One goblin was squirting dishwashing soap 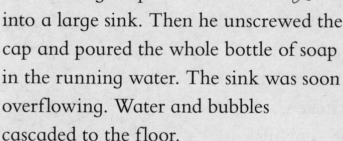 into a large sink. Then he unscrewed the cap and poured the whole bottle of soap in the running water. The sink was soon overflowing. Water and bubbles cascaded to the floor.

Clumps of pink, round bubbles floated in the air. The goblins swatted at them, slipping in the bubbles and knocking into one another.

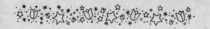

"The bag of jelly-bean cans is right there," Addison said, pointing to a metal rack that held clean glasses and plates. "The goblins seem to have forgotten about it."

Rachel knew she could reach it. She just needed to take three steps into the kitchen, without the goblins seeing her. The kitchen floor was flooded now. The soap

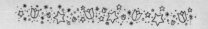

bubbles crept toward Rachel's toes.

"Here goes," Rachel whispered.
She took one step.
She could feel the
soapy water ooze
into her shoes. She
took another step,
but she was still too
far away to grab the
bag. She took one
last step. Just as she
reached out, she
heard a nasty
gasp.

"It's those pesky
girls!" a goblin
cried. At once, they
started to throw giant

handfuls of bubbles at Rachel.

Kirsty rushed in to help her, sliding in the soapy water. Bubbles flew everywhere, and soon Kirsty and Rachel couldn't even see!

Sneaky Snakes

Kirsty tried to brush the bubbles away from her face. They were everywhere!

"Rachel, Addison, are you there?" she called out. She could only see bubbles.

"Yes, right behind you," her friends replied.

Kirsty reached out and felt for the metal rack, the one with the jelly-bean

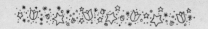

bag on it. She tried to grab on to it, but she stepped on a patch of dishwashing soap. "Ooooh!" Kirsty yelled as her feet flew into the air. She landed on the hard ground with a *thump*.

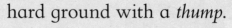

"Ha, ha, ha!" the goblins cackled when they heard her fall. One of them ran past the girls, out into the seating area.

Kirsty saw dark splotches, and then blurry versions of Rachel and Addison appeared.

"You poor thing!" Addison comforted Kirsty.

"Hey! Cookies!" the goblin yelled from the

cafeteria. "They're just sitting on a table!"

The rest of the goblins grunted and shoved one another as they raced out the kitchen door. They were all eager to eat the cookies.

"Mmmm, they look really good!" a goblin declared.

"Too bad they're all mine," insisted another as he pushed ahead of his friends.

Kirsty managed to sit up. The bubbles were popping now, and the friends could all see again. "The bag!" Kirsty said. "This is our chance!" Once the bag of jelly-bean cans was in her grasp, Kirsty felt instantly better. She loosened the drawstring and the three friends peeked inside.

Rachel gasped. "Look at all of them!"

"There are so many," Addison agreed. "I can't tell which one is my magic can."

Rachel glanced up at the clock.

"Recess is almost over," she said. "I don't think we can figure it out before we have to go back to class."

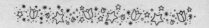

"We need lots of time or lots of hands," Kirsty said.

"Great idea, Kirsty! I have a plan," Rachel announced, "but we have to hurry."

The girls grabbed the bag and rushed out of the school kitchen, followed by Addison. They tiptoed through the cafeteria, past the goblins.

"What if they notice us?" Kirsty worried out loud. But the greedy troublemakers were too busy gobbling down toothpaste cookies to care.

Rachel and Kirsty lingered in the doorway of the girls' bathroom. Addison

was safely inside Rachel's pocket once again. As their classmates passed, Rachel and Kirsty joined the back of the line. No one had even realized that they missed recess!

The students hung their spring jackets in their cubbies and went to their seats.

"Hey, what's this?" Malcolm asked, holding up a jelly-bean can. "It was just sitting on my desk." Rachel and Kirsty smiled at each other. With Addison's help, they had quickly put a can on each desk before everyone had made it inside.

"I have one, too," Madeleine announced.

"Me, too," a whole group of kids said in chorus.

"Maybe they're from Ms. Hilaria?"
Steffi suggested. Their teacher had
stepped out of the room for a moment.
She was talking with another teacher in
the hall.

"I'm opening mine," a girl with pigtails
said. A lot of other kids agreed.

"No, you should wait until Ms. Hilaria
comes back," Steffi protested.

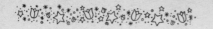

Addison sighed. "They have to try! We won't know which one is mine until it's opened."

Fortunately, no one listened to Steffi. Everyone began twisting the lids off their jelly-bean cans.

"The lid isn't coming off," Malcolm said, struggling with his can.

"It's glued shut or something," complained a girl in the back row. Rachel and Kirsty both tried theirs. They did not open. The girls looked around the room. They had been so sure one of these cans belonged to Addison. This was awful!

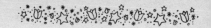

"I wonder what we should do," Kirsty whispered to Rachel.

Just then, a scream filled the room. Everyone turned to look at Steffi. She had a can in one hand, a lid in the other, and a dozen colorful streamers 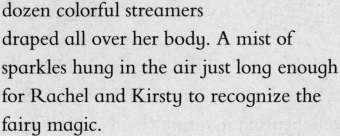 draped all over her body. A mist of sparkles hung in the air just long enough for Rachel and Kirsty to recognize the fairy magic.

The class burst out in laughter. But Steffi didn't think it was so funny. "Ms. Hilaria!" she yelled.

Ms. Hilaria rushed back into the classroom.

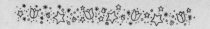

"Someone played a trick on me!"

Ms. Hilaria bit her lip as she hurried to Steffi's desk. Ms. Hilaria placed the can, lid, and streamers on an empty desk as she tried to reassure Steffi. With all the excitement, no one noticed Addison swoop in and claim her magic can. It sank to fairy size as soon as she touched it. The fairy waved happily to Rachel and Kirsty before disappearing in a tiny cloud of sparkles.

Steffi was still upset.

Kirsty looked at her with sympathy. She felt bad that Steffi couldn't enjoy the silliness of April Fool's Day.

"You know," Rachel began, "if

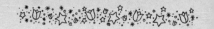

Addison had her magic key, Steffi would have been able to laugh at herself."

"You're right," Kirsty agreed. "I guess we'll just have to find Addison's key so that everyone can have a fun April Fool's Day."

The Key to
the Holiday

Contents

A Scary Discovery

"I think it will be easy to find the key," Rachel whispered to Kirsty. She shielded her mouth as she spoke, hoping the teacher would not hear her.

"Why would you say that?" Kirsty asked. "It seems like bad luck."

"I don't think you have to worry,"

Rachel said. "April Fool's Day is almost back on track."

It was true. Addison had only left the classroom a few minutes before, but the change was obvious. Ever since the fairy had taken her jelly-bean can back to Fairyland, pranks were working again—and people were laughing at them.

"Yes," Kirsty agreed. "It's very important. We need that key."

"Rachel and Kirsty," Ms. Hilaria called from the front of the class. "Please pay attention. I'm explaining our science project."

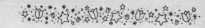

The girls immediately stopped whispering and listened to the teacher. The class was studying food groups. Ms. Hilaria had put lots of different kinds of foods on the back table. The kids were making a chart of which group the foods came from. The teacher called on them one at a time.

A boy named Jonah went first. "This graham cracker is made of wheat," he said, looking at the box. "Wheat's a plant. There are lots of other things listed here, too."

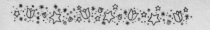

"Wheat is good for now," Ms. Hilaria said. "Thank you, Jonah."

Kirsty and Rachel filled in their charts.

Next it was Steffi's turn. As she walked to the back of the classroom to choose a food item, Malcolm leaned over to Rachel. "I carved a hole in an apple and stuck  a gummy worm inside," he said.

"That's a great April Fool's joke," Rachel told him. "I hope it works."

Steffi paused by the food table. It looked like she was going to choose the block of Swiss cheese, but she grabbed Malcolm's apple at the last second.

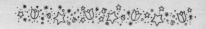

Rachel saw Malcolm cross his fingers.

"This is an apple," Steffi said. "It's a— ewww, ewww, ewww! It's a giant worm! The slimiest, bluest worm I have ever seen!"

Everyone stared at the worm, especially Malcolm. The worm squirmed around and almost touched Steffi's hand. "Ick!" she screamed, dropping the apple. It landed on the floor, and the worm wiggled out. No one laughed. Not Steffi, not even Malcolm. Everyone was in shock. It was an especially blue, very squirmy worm.

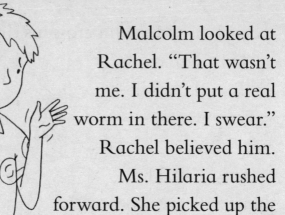

Malcolm looked at Rachel. "That wasn't me. I didn't put a real worm in there. I swear." Rachel believed him.

Ms. Hilaria rushed forward. She picked up the worm and dropped it in a pail that said COMPOST. She rinsed her hands and called on Malcolm next. His face was pale.

Kirsty raised her eyebrows. "Something funny is going on," she said.

"But not ha-ha funny," Rachel responded. "Something weird."

Just then, the girls noticed a flash of movement in the hallway. They looked closer. Two green faces were peeking into the classroom—goblins! One of them

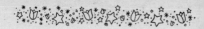

was holding a very blue, icy-looking
wand.

They knew immediately that the wand
must belong to Jack Frost! This was not
good. The goblins were never careful. If
people discovered the goblins and found
out about Fairyland, all of the girls' fairy
friends would be in danger.

"What should we do?" Kirsty asked.

Just then, they heard a light *tap, tap,*

tap. Kirsty and Rachel looked
at each other.
The noise was
coming from
inside Rachel's desk.
The girls smiled with
relief. Addison had
returned!

"Girls," the fairy
whispered, "we have
to get that wand. It's our top priority
now."

"But what about the key?" Kirsty
asked in a hushed voice.

"It will have to wait," Addison insisted.
"The goblins can do too much April
Fool's Day harm with a wand. We have
to stop them!"

Rachel and Kirsty nodded, both trying

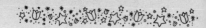

to think of a plan. Malcolm was still at the back table. He reached for the hunk of Swiss cheese and turned toward his classmates.

"This is cheese," he began.

Then a flash zigzagged across the room. An icy-blue bolt hit the cheese. Rachel knew at once that the bolt had come from the goblins' wand. What were they up to?

The Frosty Wand

"Addison, quick!" Rachel sputtered.

The fairy peeked out of the desk just in time to see the blue magic transform the cheese. It melted and re-formed into the shape of a brain. "Oh!" Addison gasped. She quickly sent a spell with her wand. When the mint-colored sparkles hit the brain, it immediately changed back to

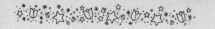

cheese. It had only been a brain for a split second, but the girls were sure that Malcolm had noticed. His face was whiter than ever. He gazed at the holey cheese in disbelief.

"Ms. Hilaria, can I go to the nurse? I don't feel very well," he said, and he set the cheese down on the table.

The teacher excused Malcolm. As he headed to the door, Rachel and Kirsty saw the goblins scurry away. "I wonder where they are going," Kirsty whispered.

"No matter where they go, they'll be up to no good," Addison said.

"All right, everyone," Ms. Hilaria said, clearing her throat. "Since Malcolm left, can someone else tell me which food group cheese comes from?"

A couple of kids raised their hands, but no one was as excited about the science unit as they had been before. There wasn't any joking, and everyone seemed bored. After discussing a few more foods, it was time for gym.

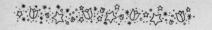

"Thank goodness!" Addison whispered. "At least we can walk through the school and see what kind of trouble the goblins have made."

The class filed into the hallway, with Rachel and Kirsty at the back of the line. "Keep your eyes out for anything suspicious," Addison advised. The fairy had squeezed herself into Rachel's sweater pocket once again.

"We will," Kirsty assured her. The girls peeked into every classroom and down every hall.

The class went through another door that was marked PUSH instead of PULL,

but it didn't fool
anyone. All the
kids were too
used to the way
the door usually
worked, so they
didn't even bother
reading the sign.

Rachel wondered what would happen
if they didn't find the key. An April
Fool's Day without jokes and laughter
was not only far from funny, it was
downright sad.

When they had almost reached the
gym, Rachel noticed Natasha's little
brother, Jake, walking down the
hallway. Just as Jake was about to pass
the girls, he bent down and reached for
the floor.

"A lucky penny!" he exclaimed.

Kirsty smiled as they passed. *It's good to see someone happy,* she thought to herself. It was only after they had turned to go into the gym that she realized the little boy was still there, kneeling over the coin. Kirsty nudged Rachel and motioned down the hall.

"Of course!" Rachel whispered when she saw Jake tugging at the coin. "The glue-the-coin-to-the-floor trick. It's a classic. The coin is stuck, so no one can pick it up."

Addison poked her head out of Rachel's pocket. "It's so nice to see a joke that's actually working. Maybe when he

realizes that it's an
April Fool's Day
prank, that boy
will be able to laugh
at himself," the fairy
said hopefully.

But as the three friends watched Jake
try to pry the coin off the floor, they
realized that something was not
right—it wasn't just the coin that was
stuck to the floor.

The girls rushed over to the little boy's
side. "Hi, Jake," Rachel said. "I'm
Rachel, one of Natasha's friends. This is
my friend Kirsty. Are you okay?"

When Jake looked up, his blue eyes were
brimming with tears. "I just wanted some
good luck, so I went to pick up the penny,"
he whimpered. "But now I'm stuck!"

Unlucky
Penny

Kirsty's eyes grew wide. Jake wasn't trying to pick up the penny—he was trying to get loose! His finger was glued to the coin. When Kirsty looked closer, she could see tiny blue ice bolts floating all around the coin. "Goblins," she muttered to herself.

Addison must have been thinking the same thing. In a flash, the fairy pointed her wand. Mint-colored magic streamed toward the penny and Jake's hand. It looped around them like a glittering bow. Fortunately, Jake was staring at his hand and didn't see her.

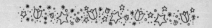

"It's all right, Jake," Rachel said when she saw the magic at work. "Try to move your hand now."

The little boy pulled his hand away with short, jerky movements. He looked at Rachel in relief. "It really was stuck," he insisted.

"I believe you," Rachel said. "I really do."

"How does it feel now?" Kirsty asked.

"It tingles," he said, "but I'm fine. I just want to go back to class." Jake immediately stood up and headed down the hall in a hurry.

"Go straight to your class, and don't pick up any more coins today!" Rachel

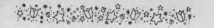

called out. With that, Jake broke into a jog, pulled open the door to the main hallway, and ran to his room without looking back.

"What a terrible trick to play!" declared Addison. "He couldn't even laugh at himself. It wasn't funny at all."

Rachel and Kirsty both shook their heads.

"The blue magic on that coin was fresh," the fairy continued. "I'm sure the goblins are near."

The three friends headed to the gym door and peered inside. Sure enough, they could see some unfamiliar kids in the class. The unfamiliar kids all wore

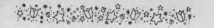

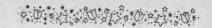

baseball caps with long bills to cover
their long noses. Those noses were all a
very familiar shade of green.

The girls joined their class in the gym.
Addison flew up and perched on a
basketball hoop where no one would see
her.

As Rachel sat down, she was amazed
that none of her classmates had noticed
the goblins. "They must have used the
wand," she whispered to Kirsty.

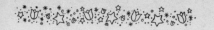

"That makes sense," Kirsty agreed. "They probably used a spell that keeps people from noticing that they're goblins."

Mr. Chen, the gym teacher, clapped his hands to get everyone's attention. "Kids, I have a big surprise for you," he began. "Today, we are playing Ping-Pong. Who here likes Ping-Pong?"

All the kids raised their hands. Next, the teacher asked, "Who has what it takes to be a Ping-Pong master?"

Before Mr. Chen had finished the question, a long-armed goblin jumped up and yelled, "ME, ME, ME!" He

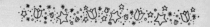

waved his hands around, and Rachel
and Kirsty gasped. Jack Frost's icy-blue
wand glittered in the gym lights.

The long-armed goblin had the wand!
The girls glanced up at Addison. They
wanted to make sure
she knew, too. The
fairy gave them a
thumbs-up.

"I'm glad you enjoy
Ping-Pong, but please
sit down," Mr. Chen said
to the goblin with the long arms. The
teacher then shared some Ping-Pong
pointers and split the kids into groups.

Kirsty looked around the gym and
realized there were six Ping-Pong tables
set up. Each group went to a separate
table.

"Too bad we didn't end up in that goblin's group," Rachel whispered to Kirsty. Instead, the girls were playing with Steffi and some boys. "My dad taught me all the rules," Steffi said to their group. "I'm really good. Just ask me if you have questions."

Kirsty nodded at Steffi. She wondered if the other girl was always so serious about everything!

"Each game is to ten points," Mr. Chen announced. "The two players with the most wins will play in a championship game. Now, let's get started!"

Ping-Pong Peril

Kirsty and Rachel could tell at once that
Steffi and the long-armed goblin were
the best players. They both served the
ball with quick snaps of their paddles.
Everyone else watched in amazement.
No one could score against either one of
them! Steffi and the long-armed goblin
quickly had several wins each.

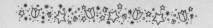

After Kirsty played Steffi, they all watched the long-armed goblin play a pointy-nosed goblin. The long-armed goblin held the wand in the same hand as his paddle, so no one could see it. The long-armed goblin finally missed a shot, but the ball didn't hit the ground. Just as it

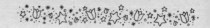

was about to hit the floor, it rose back up in the air, zoomed across the table, and smacked the pointy-nosed goblin in the belly! "Hey!" the other goblin cried. "You cheated!" Rachel realized they needed to get the wand, and fast. None of their classmates had noticed how the goblin was winning, but it was only a matter of time.

Out of the corner of her eye, Rachel saw Addison. The fairy pointed to the gym teacher's office. Rachel grabbed

Kirsty's hand. "Addison wants us to go in there," she said.

Kirsty smiled. "She must have a plan."

A short time later, three fairies fluttered out of the gym office. Addison had explained her idea to the girls. She wanted to turn them into fairies so they could more easily search for her key. The two friends flapped their new glittery wings and tried to keep up with Addison.

Down on the gym floor, the last game of Ping-Pong had begun. It was Steffi against the long-armed goblin. "The winner gets a medal," Mr. Chen announced. "You will be today's Ping-Pong champion."

The three fairies watched from their perch on the basketball hoop. The goblin

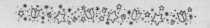

had a greedy smile. "That medal is mine," he said with a sneer. At the other end of the table, Steffi waited for the goblin's serve.

The goblin served the ball. It zoomed right past Steffi, leaving a trail of blue bolts. The goblin did a cartwheel to celebrate his first point. As he flipped over, a shiny necklace fell out of his shirt. "It's my magic key!" Addison exclaimed. "The same goblin has the wand *and* the key. How do we get them?"

"What if Kirsty and I distract him?" Rachel suggested. "Then you can grab the wand."

"And hopefully the key, too," Kirsty added. "But won't the other kids notice us?"

"Not if they can't see you," Addison said. Kirsty looked at the fairy, confused. "I can make you invisible. At least for a little while," Addison explained. "What do you think?"

Kirsty and Rachel looked at each other and nodded. With a tap of her wand, Addison sent a swirl of sparkles around the three fairies.

Kirsty waved to her best friend as her hand—and the rest of her—began to disappear. Now she could only see faint outlines of Rachel and Addison. "No one

will be able to see
us!" she said, and
they flew toward the
center Ping-Pong
table.

The goblin had nine
points, and Steffi had zero.

"He's so good!" one of the kids
exclaimed.

"He's going to win," another agreed.

The rest of the goblins all cheered from
the crowd.

Kirsty was frustrated. *The goblin doesn't
deserve to win,* she thought. *He's not playing
fair.* She flew close to the goblin and
tickled him behind the ear. Rachel flew
close to his other ear. The goblin swatted
at his head. When Steffi served the ball
to him, he missed.

"Ooof!" the goblin cried. "That's not fair. I have a bug in my ear."

The goblin waved his hands all over, but Kirsty and Rachel dodged them. Soon, the score was tied. Both Steffi and the goblin had nine points. Steffi served the ball, and the goblin grunted as it zoomed past him.

"Congratulations, Steffi," Mr. Chen called out. "That's ten points. You win!"

Mr. Chen placed a shiny gold-colored medal around her neck, and Steffi smiled.

"No! No! No!" yelled the goblin. "I want that medal." With his long arms, the goblin reached out and snatched the medal right from Steffi's neck. Then he ran straight out of the gym.

Party
Prank

"Hey!" cried Steffi. "I worked hard for that." She took off after the goblin. The rest of the goblins ran after her, and the three fairies followed them. Soon, they were all racing out of the gym and down the hallway.

"The goblin still has the wand and the key!" Addison called to the girls. "I couldn't grab either of them."

"We'll get them," Kirsty said, but she wasn't sure how.

The long-armed goblin glanced over his shoulder. He was close to the door at the end of the hallway. Steffi was just two steps behind him. The goblin put out his hands to push open the door, but it didn't budge. He ran smack into it! Steffi couldn't stop herself in time and ran into him. Then the crowd of goblins jumbled into them.

The fairies watched in amazement as the wand flew out of the goblin's hand in one direction and the magical golden key flew out in another.

"Quick!" Addison yelled. "I'll get the wand. You two grab the key!" The girls rushed forward and caught the key in midair. Addison claimed the wand.

Rachel and Kirsty carried the key over to Addison, who was tucked away in a hidden doorway. The invisible magic had worn off, so they needed to be careful again. As they handed the key to the fairy, it shrank down to its Fairyland size. "Oh, thank you, girls," Addison said. "It's time for me to take this wand and the key back to where they belong."

Steffi and the goblins were starting to help one another up.

"What happened?" the long-armed goblin asked, dazed.

Steffi started to giggle. "You fell for that April Fool's Day joke," she said, pointing at the door. "You pushed, but the sign is wrong. You have to pull!" Steffi bent over laughing. "April Fool's!" she called out.

The goblins stared at the door, slowly realizing what had happened.

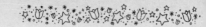

At first, the goblin with the long arms looked annoyed, but then a smile pulled at the corners of his mouth. "Who changed that sign?" he mumbled. "We must have looked pretty funny!" His laughter burst out like a trumpet.

"*You* changed the sign, silly!" one of the goblins said, slapping the long-armed goblin on the shoulder.

Kirsty looked at Steffi and the goblins, all laughing at themselves. "I think the key's magic is starting to work already."

"Yes," Addison agreed. "Isn't it wonderful? Thanks for all your help. I

don't know how
I will ever repay you."

"We're just happy
that April Fool's Day
will be fun again,"
Rachel said.

Addison waved
her wand to change Rachel and Kirsty
back into human girls. Then she blew
them each a kiss and vanished in a
sparkly, mint-colored cloud.

They stepped out of the doorway and
gasped. The long-armed goblin was
giving the Ping-Pong medal back to
Steffi!

"Thank you," Steffi said.

"You won it, fair and square," the
goblin admitted.

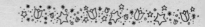

"Maybe we'll get a rematch one day," Steffi said.

"Maybe," the runner-up replied.

The small group headed back to the gym, where Ms. Hilaria was waiting for them. "Class, we have to get back to the room," the teacher said with a sly grin. "I planned a pop quiz on the food groups for you."

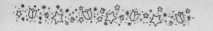

The kids all grumbled and lined up to go back to class.

Rachel and Kirsty joined Steffi at the back of the line.

"A pop quiz?" Steffi wondered. "That's not a very fun way to end April Fool's Day."

"Maybe not," Rachel replied, "but I'll bet Ms. Hilaria can make it pretty fun." Steffi gave her a confused look and turned back around. The kids shuffled down the hall behind their teacher. No one was in a hurry to take a quiz. But when Ms. Hilaria opened the classroom door, they were in for a surprise.

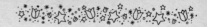

The whole room was decorated with streamers and balloons. There were all kinds of treats on the back table, including containers of jelly beans!

"This room looks incredible," Kirsty said.

"It's almost magical," Rachel agreed. "I wonder if Ms. Hilaria had some extra-special help."

"Maybe," Kirsty said, popping a jelly bean in her mouth. Just then, Steffi came up to the two friends. "Hey, Rachel. Did you know that Ms. Hilaria had planned this party?" she asked.

"Not really," Rachel answered. "But I did think telling us we were having a pop quiz would be a good April Fool's Day joke."

"That's true," Steffi said. "She certainly tricked me. I forgot how much fun April Fool's Day can be!"

With that, Rachel and Kirsty smiled at each other.

"Want some jelly beans?" Kirsty asked.

"Sure," Rachel said. She twisted the lid

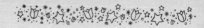

off the jelly-bean can, and streamers
came flying out.

"April Fool's!" Kirsty called.

Steffi grinned and plucked a streamer
off of Rachel's shoulder.

Rachel shook her head. "I can't believe
I fell for that!" All she could do was
laugh—and that was a good thing.

SPECIAL EDITION

Don't miss any of Rachel and Kirsty's
other fairy adventures!
Join them as they try to help

Bailey

the Babysitter Fairy!

Read on for a special sneak peek. . . .

Vacation Begins!

"Rachel, look!" Kirsty Tate gasped, peeking out of the lodge window. "We can see the butterfly house from our bedroom!"

Rachel Walker dropped her suitcase and ran around to the other side of the bed. As soon as she pulled back the polka-dot print curtain, her face lit up with a smile.

"I can see it!" she replied. There, almost hidden among the trees, was a cluster of cabins and greenhouses in all different shapes and sizes. The butterfly house was the one in the middle, next to the main eco-center. Inside, tropical plants and flowers curled up toward the sunshine, filling the dome with rainbow colors.

It was the perfect beginning to the girls' spring break. Kirsty and Rachel had only just arrived, but they loved it here already! Their families had organized this weekend away at the EcoWorld activity center—an amazing park set in the heart of a leafy forest. Mr. and Mrs. Tate's friends, the Robinsons, had been invited, too.

Everything at EcoWorld had been

carefully designed to protect the animals
and plants that lived in the countryside
around it. The Tates, Walkers, and
Robinsons were spending the weekend in
a pretty eco-lodge built out of reclaimed
wood. Everything in the park was
recycled, even the water in the
swimming pools!

Kirsty picked up her EcoWorld
brochure and started flicking through the
pages.

"Should we go exploring?" she asked.
"It says there's a climbing wall and a
rainforest area and . . . wow! Rachel, the
dome with the man-made lake has a
roof that opens up when its sunny!"

Rachel couldn't help but giggle—she'd
grabbed her fleece already! She and
Kirsty had only three precious days

together and she wanted to make the
most of every minute.

"I wonder what we'll find today?" she
mused.

Kirsty's eyes twinkled. She and Rachel
were used to discovering all kinds of
amazing, magical things. The lucky girls
shared a secret—they were friends with
the fairies! The pair had been on some
incredible adventures. Jack Frost and his
goblins were always stomping into
Fairyland and trying to stir up trouble. If
a fairy needed their help, they only had
to wave their magic wand and Rachel
and Kirsty would be there.

The girls slipped on their fleeces and
scampered out into the yard. The lodge
had large glass doors that opened onto a
daisy-speckled lawn.

"Kirsty! Kirsty!" chimed a little voice.

"Play! Play!" piped up another.

Kirsty and Rachel beamed at each other. The friends moved aside the branches of a pretty weeping willow and spotted Tom and Lily, Mr. and Mrs. Robinson's two-year-old twins. The toddlers were playing in a sandbox made out of recycled railroad ties.

"Hello, you two!" exclaimed Kirsty. "This is my best friend, Rachel."

"Ra-ra," cooed Lily.

Rachel bent down to meet the excited twins. Lily played peekaboo behind her hands, but Tom gave her a wide smile.

Tom glanced at Lily, then shyly presented their new friend with a shiny orange shovel.

"We can't play right now, Tom," Kirsty

said kindly, "but we'll come back and build sandcastles later."

Rachel nodded. "We just want to see what there is to do in EcoWorld."

The adorable little boy clapped his hands. He'd spotted Mrs. Tate wandering up to the sandbox with his bottle. Kirsty's mom pulled a crumpled list and some money out of her jeans pocket.

"Can you pick me up a few things from the supermarket?" she asked. "Just follow the signs. The park is totally enclosed, so you can't get lost. Use the change to treat yourselves to a shake at the café afterwards if you want."

"Great!" Kirsty grinned.

She linked arms with Rachel, steering her toward a path at the bottom of the garden.

"Isn't this amazing?" remarked Rachel, as the friends stepped onto a maze of boardwalks. Every so often, the walkway would turn a corner revealing a building nestled in the trees.

The friends rushed to the supermarket and picked out Mrs. Tate's groceries. Soon they were sitting in the Treetop Café, each clutching a tasty milkshake.

"I'll get some straws," offered Kirsty, spotting a container in the corner.

She lifted the lid and picked out two straws with glittering stripes. She took them back to the table.

Rachel blinked, then peered around the café. Was she imagining it, or did her straw seem to be sparkling more brightly than everyone else's?

RAINBOW magic™

SPECIAL EDITION

Don't miss any of Rachel and Kirsty's
other fairy adventures!
Check out this magical sneak peek of

Keira

the Movie Star Fairy!

Setting the Scene

"Look, there's Julianna Stewart!" whispered Kirsty Tate. "Isn't her fairy princess costume beautiful?"

Rachel Walker peeked around just as Julianna walked past. The movie star gave the girls a friendly wink, then sat down in a director's chair with her name on the back to study her script.

"I can't believe a really famous actress like Julianna would come to Wetherbury village," said Rachel.

"And I can't believe that she's spending most of our school vacation in Mrs. Croft's garden!" added Kirsty.

Mrs. Croft was a friend of Kirsty's parents, a sweet old lady who had lived in Wetherbury for years. Her little thatched cottage with pretty, blossoming trees in the front yard often caught the eyes of tourists and passersby. A few weeks ago when Mrs. Croft had been working in her garden, an executive from a big movie studio had pulled up outside. He wanted to use the cottage in a brand-new movie starring the famous actress Julianna Stewart. When Mrs. Croft agreed, she became the talk of the village! Trucks full of set designers, lighting engineers, and prop-makers had turned up to transform her garden into a magical world. Now, filming on *The Starlight Chronicles* was about to begin.

"It was so nice of Mrs. Croft to let us spend some time on the set," said Rachel, watching the director talk through the next scene with his star.

Not only had Mrs. Croft arranged for the friends to watch the rehearsals, but when she'd heard that Rachel was coming to stay with Kirsty for a week, the kind old lady had also managed to get the girls parts as extras!

The pair had been cast as magical fairies, helpers to Julianna's fairy princess in one of the most exciting scenes in the movie. It was the perfect part for them both — Kirsty and Rachel knew a lot about fairies! The two best friends had been secretly visiting Fairyland for a while. They never knew when one of the fairies would need their help, but they were always ready to protect their magical friends from Jack Frost and his troublesome goblins.

"I can't wait to try on our costumes," said Kirsty. "I wonder if they'll be as beautiful as real fairy clothes."

Rachel shook her head and smiled. All the sequins and glitter in the human world couldn't look as magical as a real fairy fluttering in her finery! Before she could answer her friend, the director tapped his clipboard with a pen.

"Attention, everybody," he called. "I'd like to run this scene from the top. We start filming first thing tomorrow and there's still lots of work to do."

Kirsty and Rachel exchanged excited looks as the set bustled with people. Helpers known as "runners" got props for the actors and showed the extras where to stand. Sound and lighting experts rigged up cables, while the dancers practiced their steps. In this scene of *The Starlight Chronicles*, the fairy princess was due to greet the prince at a sparkling moonlit ball.

Kirsty and Rachel couldn't wait to hear the stars run through their lines! They watched as Julianna took her place in front of Chad Stenning, the actor cast as the fairy prince.

"And . . . action!" cried the director, giving a thumbs-up.

Julianna coughed shyly, then stepped forward.

"Your Highness," she said, making a dainty curtsy. "The air shimmers with enchantment this evening. Shall we dance?"

Chad bowed. "Let the music wait a while. Please walk with me on the terrace. There is something I must say."

The crew watched, spellbound, as Chad offered his arm to Julianna and led her off the set.

"Excellent work!" announced the director, making a note on his clipboard. "Let's take five."

Rachel and Kirsty chatted while the cast took a quick break. Runners rushed around the director, collecting notes and passing messages to the crew.

"I haven't seen that runner before," whispered Rachel, nudging her friend's arm. "He seems to be in a big hurry."

Kirsty looked up as the runner elbowed his way past the actors, then snatched a script from the director's table. She tried to see his face, but it was hidden under a dark baseball cap. It was only when he bumped her chair on the way out of the garden that she spotted a glimpse of green skin.

"That's no runner," Kirsty said breathlessly. "It's a goblin!"

★   ★   ★

Rachel felt the back of her neck begin to tingle. If Jack Frost's goblins were in Wetherbury, it could mean nothing but trouble! She followed Kirsty's gaze and saw that, sure enough, two warty green feet were poking out of the bottom of the stranger's jeans.

"That's a goblin all right," she said. "We'd better follow him!"

Kirsty nodded and jumped to her feet, just as the director called "Action!" one more time. Before the girls could slip away, a group of actors rushed forward to act out a party scene in the enchanted garden.

"Good evening, Your Highness," piped up a girl in a fairy skirt.

The man next to her elbowed the girl in the ribs and hissed, "That's *my* line, silly!"

The director rolled his eyes. "Take it from the top, please."

"Attention, fairies! Sinner is derved," babbled the man. "Oh, no! I mean 'dinner is served'! Or does that line come later? I can't remember!"

"Let's move on." The director frowned, turning to Chad and Julianna.

The cast and crew waited for the leading man and lady to start speaking. But instead of saying their lines, they stayed totally silent.

"Julianna?" called the director. "Julianna!"

Julianna looked helplessly at Chad.

"Is it m–me next?" she stuttered. "My mind's gone blank!"

The set fell into chaos as assistants scrambled to track down the correct page in the script.

"I don't understand," whispered Rachel. "Chad and Julianna have been perfect up until now. Something has gone terribly wrong."

"We have to find that goblin! I bet he has something to do with all this," Kirsty said.

Rachel pointed to a path made of stepping-stones that curved around the back of Mrs. Croft's cottage. "He ran down there. Let's go!"

RAINBOW magic™

SPECIAL EDITION

Which Magical Fairies Have You Met?

3 stories in each one!

- ☐ Joy the Summer Vacation Fairy
- ☐ Holly the Christmas Fairy
- ☐ Kylie the Carnival Fairy
- ☐ Stella the Star Fairy
- ☐ Shannon the Ocean Fairy
- ☐ Trixie the Halloween Fairy
- ☐ Gabriella the Snow Kingdom Fairy
- ☐ Juliet the Valentine Fairy
- ☐ Mia the Bridesmaid Fairy
- ☐ Flora the Dress-Up Fairy
- ☐ Paige the Christmas Play Fairy
- ☐ Emma the Easter Fairy
- ☐ Cara the Camp Fairy
- ☐ Destiny the Rock Star Fairy
- ☐ Belle the Birthday Fairy
- ☐ Olympia the Games Fairy
- ☐ Selena the Sleepover Fairy
- ☐ Cheryl the Christmas Tree Fairy
- ☐ Florence the Friendship Fairy
- ☐ Lindsay the Luck Fairy
- ☐ Brianna the Tooth Fairy
- ☐ Autumn the Falling Leaves Fairy
- ☐ Keira the Movie Star Fairy
- ☐ Addison the April Fool's Day Fairy

📖 SCHOLASTIC

Find all of your favorite fairy friends at
scholastic.com/rainbowmagic

RMSPECIAL12

RAINBOW magic™

Which Magical Fairies Have You Met?

- ☐ The Rainbow Fairies
- ☐ The Weather Fairies
- ☐ The Jewel Fairies
- ☐ The Pet Fairies
- ☐ The Dance Fairies
- ☐ The Music Fairies
- ☐ The Sports Fairies
- ☐ The Party Fairies
- ☐ The Ocean Fairies
- ☐ The Night Fairies
- ☐ The Magical Animal Fairies
- ☐ The Princess Fairies
- ☐ The Superstar Fairies
- ☐ The Fashion Fairies
- ☐ The Sugar & Spice Fairies

■ SCHOLASTIC

Find all of your favorite fairy friends at
scholastic.com/rainbowmagic

RMFAIRY9

RAINBOW magic™

These activities are magical!
Play dress-up, send friendship notes, and much more!

■SCHOLASTIC

www.scholastic.com
www.rainbowmagiconline.com

HIT entertainment

RMACTIV3